Pokémon

Words and Music by John Loeffler (A...

Rap:

So you wanna be a master of
POKÉMON
Understand the Secrets and
HAVE SOME FUN
So you wanna be a master of Pokémon
POKÉMON
Do you have the skills to be
NUMBER ONE?

Verse I:

I wanna take the ultimate step
Find the courage to be bold
To risk it all and not forget
The lessons that I hold

I wanna go where no one's been
Far beyond the crowd
Learn the way to take command
Use the power that's in my hand

Chorus:

We all live in a Pokémon World
I want to be the greatest master of them all
We all live in a Pokémon World
Put myself to the test
Be better than all the rest

Verse II:

Every day along the way
I will be prepared
With every challenge I will gain
Knowledge to be shared

In my heart there's no doubt
Of who I want to be
Right here standing strong
The greatest Master of Pokémon

Chorus:

Rap: You've got the power right in your hands

There are more books about Pokémon.

Collect them all!

POKéMON
THE JOHTO JOURNEYS

The Chikorita Challenge

Adapted by Tracey West

SCHOLASTIC INC.
New York   Toronto   London   Auckland   Sydney
Mexico City   New Delhi   Hong Kong

JOHTO LEAGUE

ISBN 0-439-22113-7

12 11 10 9   10/0

Printed in the U.S.A.
First Scholastic printing, June 2001

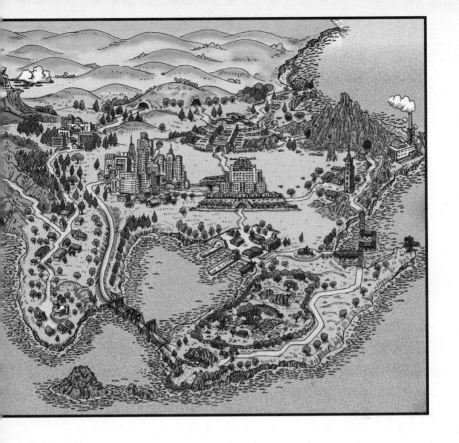

Who's That Pokémon?

Ash Ketchum had been a Pokémon trainer ever since his tenth birthday.

Since then, Ash had gone on incredible adventures. He'd traveled to faraway places and seen many strange and unusual Pokémon.

But he'd never seen anything quite like Chikorita.

The first time he spotted a real Chikorita, Ash was traveling through the West. As usual, his friends Brock and Misty walked by his side. Brock, an older boy, had dark hair. Orange-haired Misty always carried around Togepi, a Pokémon that still wore a colorful eggshell.

Like the others, Ash carried his Pokémon in red-and-white Poké Balls — all but one. Pikachu, a yellow Electric Pokémon, liked to walk at Ash's side. Pikachu had become Ash's closest friend.

But like any good Pokémon trainer, Ash was always looking for new Pokémon to catch and train. He was daydreaming about his next catch as they walked through a small town. Then a loud voice brought him back to reality.

"Go, go, Chikorita! Knock 'em down! Knock 'em down!"

The voice belonged to a young girl. She wore a yellow-and-black baseball shirt and cap. Her name, Casey, was spelled out on the back of the shirt.

Casey was standing in a park up ahead. In front of her stood a small green Grass Pokémon. A green leaf grew out of the top of its head. A ring of green dots circled its neck.

"Look, it's a Chikorita," Misty said.

Ash switched on Dexter, his Pokédex. Ash had seen a picture of Chikorita before, but he wanted more information. Dexter, a handheld computer, would have just what he needed.

"Chikorita, the leaf Pokémon, is able to release a subtle, sweet fragrance from the leaves on its head," Dexter said.

Ash still wasn't satisfied. To really learn about Chikorita, he'd have to see it in action.

It looked like that's exactly what Casey had in mind. Ash saw a Rattata run out from a bush in the park. The wild Pokémon looked like a furry brown rat.

"She's going to use Chikorita to catch that Rattata," Brock remarked. "She must be a new trainer."

Ash knew Brock was right. Rattata were easy to catch.

Casey started to talk like a sports announcer. "Chikorita is pitching for Team

Casey. With a wild Rattata at bat, Chikorita is looking to strike out the other team. Chikorita, Tackle!"

Ash couldn't believe it. Casey was acting like she was at a baseball game. What did baseball have to do with Pokémon?

Her Chikorita didn't seem to care. It sped toward the Rattata. The wild Pokémon quickly dodged the attack.

Casey wasn't concerned. "Ah, the first pitch is a ball, but Chikorita goes into a second windup! One more Tackle, Chikorita. Go!"

Chikorita ran at the Rattata once again. This time, the leaf Pokémon made contact. The Tackle knocked Rattata to the ground.

Casey jumped up and down. "That does it! Chikorita's attack has broken down Rattata. Now I'll catch it!"

Ash knew Casey had to make her move quickly, while the Rattata was weak.

She did. She threw out a Poké Ball. The ball opened up in front of Rattata. A white light shot out. The Rattata disappeared, and the ball closed.

Casey picked up the Poké Ball and held it up high. "I caught you, Rattata!" she cried.

Casey put Chikorita back into its Poké Ball. Then she started to hop up and down, chanting a baseball cheer.

Ash decided it was time to introduce himself. Casey might be embarassed if she knew anyone was watching her. He knew he would be.

"Ahem!" Ash said.

Casey stopped and turned around. She didn't look embarassed at all. Her eyes lit up when she saw Pikachu. She ran over and grabbed the little yellow Pokémon.

"A Pikachu! I can't believe it," Casey said.

"That's my Pikachu," Ash said, a little stiffly. "My name is Ash Ketchum. I'm from Pallet Town."

Casey held out her hand. "My name's Casey. I just started my Pokémon journey. I got a Chikorita from Professor Elm in New Bark Town."

Brock and Misty introduced themselves. Casey had a hard time taking her eyes off Pikachu.

"I can't help it, I just love Pikachu," Casey said. "I love its fluffy yellow body, the stripes on its back, the black tips on its ears . . ."

"Pikachu matches your uniform," Misty said.

"That's right," Casey said. "I love all yellow Pokémon, especially if they have stripes. Electabuzz is the best. My dream is to have my own team of striped yellow Pokémon."

"Why are you so hung up on yellow and stripes?" Ash asked.

Casey pointed to the uniform. "The Electabuzz baseball team. They're the greatest. Everyone in my family loves them."

"The Electabuzz?" Ash said. "But they rank last every year. What's the point of rooting for a losing team? I'd go for the Magikarp team myself."

Casey looked angry. "The Electabuzz will beat them this year. I know they will!"

Ash shrugged. "Whatever you say. I just don't think they have much of a chance."

Casey's face turned bright red. "I can't listen anymore," she said. She reached into her pocket and took out a Poké Ball.

"What are you doing?" Ash asked.

"I'm challenging you," Casey said firmly. "Let's end this argument with a Pokémon battle!"

2

The Rookie Chikorita

"I can't battle you," Ash said. "You're just starting out. It wouldn't be fair."

Casey looked determined. "What's the matter? Are you afraid you'll be beaten by a rookie?"

That was all Ash needed to hear. "Fine. You want to battle? Let's battle!"

Misty sighed. "I can't believe these two are going to battle over which baseball team is best," she told Brock.

Casey and Ash faced each other across the park.

9

"Let's use three Pokémon each," Casey said.

"Whatever you say," Ash replied.

"Don't be too hard on her, Ash," Brock said. "Remember, she's new at this."

"Someone's got to teach her how rough battling can be," Ash answered. He turned to Casey. "You can attack first."

Casey threw a Poké Ball into the air. "Batting first for Casey will be — Pidgey!"

A brown Pokémon burst from the ball. Ash smiled.

"I remember when I caught my first Pidgey," he said. "It seems like so long ago now."

"Quit babbling and bring it on!" Casey snapped.

Ash couldn't take any more. Somebody had to put Casey in her place.

Ash tossed a Poké Ball. There was a flash of white light, and a huge orange Pokémon appeared. Charizard, a combination Fire and Flying Pokémon, towered over Ash and Casey. Compared to Charizard, Pidgey seemed harmless.

"I can't believe Ash chose Charizard," Misty said. "It isn't fair. Pidgey doesn't stand a chance!"

Casey heard her. "I won't back down," she said. "Pidgey, Quick Attack!"

Pidgey flew right at Charizard. The brown Pokémon slammed into Charizard's big belly. Pidgey bounced off and landed on the ground.

Charizard snorted, and fire came out of its nostrils. Then it knocked Pidgey with its long tail, sending the Pokémon sailing back to Casey.

Casey held out a Poké Ball. "Pidgey, return. Looks like my second batter is up. Rattata, Tackle!"

Rattata burst from the Poké Ball. The furry Pokémon ran at Charizard with all its might.

Rattata slammed into Charizard's belly, too. The small Pokémon promptly fainted from the impact.

"This can't be," Casey said, shocked.

Ash grinned. "I guess I've made my point. Ready to give up now?"

Casey called Rattata back into her Poké Ball. Then she held up a third ball. "I won't quit. The game always gets more exciting once there are two outs. My third batter will be Chikorita."

The yellow leaf Pokémon popped out of the ball.

"Give me a home run, Chikorita!" Casey called out. "Use Vine Whip."

Green vines came out of two of the dots that circled Chikorita's neck. The vines lashed out and wrapped around Charizard's neck.

"All right!" cheered Casey.

Part of Ash admired Casey's confidence. Another part of Ash couldn't wait to show her who was the better trainer.

"Charizard, use Flamethrower. But go easy," he added.

Charizard grunted. The large Pokémon shot a stream of flame at the leaf on top of Chikorita's head. The leaf caught fire, and Chikorita ran around in circles to try to put out the flames. It wasn't long before the exhausted Pokémon collapsed.

"This battle is over," Brock announced. "It's a shutout for Ash."

Casey looked devastated. "Return, Chikorita," she said.

"Don't feel bad, Casey," Misty said. "You did just fine for a beginner."

Casey couldn't look at them. "I lost on my home field. There's no excuse."

Ash felt bad for her. He held out his hand. "Once the battle ends, opponents should be friends. How about it?"

But Casey ran down the road.

Ash watched her disappear around a corner. "I hope she doesn't get discouraged. She could be a really good trainer someday."

Ash wasn't the only one watching Casey. A boy and girl, and a small Pokémon spied on the girl from a hiding place on top of a tall tree. They had seen the whole battle.

The treetop spies were none other than Team Rocket, a trio of Pokémon thieves who were alway trying to steal rare Pokémon.

Jessie, the girl, swept a strand of long, red hair out of her eyes. "Are you thinking what I'm thinking?" she asked.

James, the boy, nodded. "We can use this rivalry to our advantage."

Meowth, a scratch cat Pokémon, got a gleam in its eye. "I have just the plan," Meowth said.

A short while later, Team Rocket caught

up with Casey outside of her house. They walked up to her, dressed in yellow-and-black Electabuzz baseball uniforms.

"Look! It's another Electabuzz fan," Jessie said. "But you can't possibly love the Electabuzz team as much as we do."

Casey brightened. "I sure do! They're the best team ever."

"They sure are," said James. "Hooray, Electabuzz!"

Casey eyed the three of them. "Who are you guys, anyway?" she asked.

"We're just some Electabuzz fans who happened to be passing by," Jessie said innocently. "We caught your last battle."

Casey hung her head. "I'm so embarassed. I lost big time."

"But that's not your fault," Meowth said. "What else could you do against that infamous criminal, Ash Ketchum?"

Casey looked puzzled. "Ash is a bad guy?"

"The baddest guy there is," James said. "He's a big cheater. I bet he cheated you in that last battle."

"What?" Casey said, "I won't let him get away with it!"

"That's the spirit!" Jessie said. "I think he's still in town. You should challenge him to another battle right now."

Casey started to run down the street. "I'll do it. I have to defend my honor, and the honor of Electabuzz fans everywhere!"

When Casey was out of sight, Team Rocket broke into laughter.

"My plan is working perfectly," Jessie said. "That little twerp won't be able to resist Casey's challenge. The second battle will weaken their Pokémon. Then we'll be able to swoop in and swipe them all."

"Hey, that's *my* plan!" Meowth said angrily.

James straightened the baseball cap on his head. "It doesn't matter whose plan it was," he said. "Let's get going. We've got some Pokémon to steal!"

Battle on the Ball Field

Ash faced Casey in the middle of a baseball field. Brock, Misty, and Togepi watched them from the stands.

Ash couldn't believe Casey had asked him for a rematch. He thought he had taught her a lesson with Charizard. But she wanted another battle, and Ash never turned down a challenger.

"You won't beat me so easily this time," Casey said confidently. Then she began to talk like a sports announcer again. "Casey's

team is up to bat. Her first Pokémon will be . . . Chikorita!"

"Chikorita, huh?" Ash said. Charizard had taken care of Chikorita easily. He knew Pikachu would do the same.

"I choose you, Pikachu," Ash told his Pokémon.

Pikachu nodded and stepped in front of Ash. Chikorita stood at Casey's side.

"Last time, I used my fastball," Casey said. "Now it's time to throw a curveball. Chikorita, Sweet Smell!"

Casey's command startled Ash. He had never heard of an attack called Sweet Smell. What would Chikorita do?

The leaf on top of Chikorita's head swirled around. A strange odor wafted up and tickled Ash's nose. He could see that Pikachu was affected, too.

Ash found that the smell was all he could think of. He forgot all about the battle. He even forgot he was standing in a ballfield.

"Now, Chikorita, Tackle!" Casey cried. Ash heard her command, but felt like he couldn't do anything to stop it.

Chikorita raced across the field.

Slam! Chikorita's Tackle knocked over Pikachu.

"We did it!" Casey cheered. "One more time, Chikorita."

The effect of the Sweet Smell Attack wore off. Ash tried to shake the dazed feeling out of his head. Was Pikachu okay?

Pikachu stood up. It would take more than a Tackle to keep down Ash's best Poké-mon.

"Not so fast, Casey," Ash said. "Pikachu, Thunderbolt!"

As Pikachu built up the electric charge for the attack, Misty and Brock watched, worried.

"What is Ash doing?" Misty wondered.

Brock shook his head. "Chikorita is

Grass Pokémon," he said. "Grass Pokémon are strong against Electric Attacks. Ash knows that."

But Ash had forgotten. Pikachu launched into the Thunderbolt Attack.

Boom! The yellow Pokémon hurled a blast of electric energy at Chikorita. Casey's Pokémon reacted quickly. It waved one of the leaves on top of its head. The leaf deflected the charge, sending it safely into the dirt.

"Now, Chikorita!" Casey yelled. "Another Tackle!"

Still weak from launching its attack, Pikachu didn't have a chance to escape the Tackle. Ash cringed as Pikachu fell to the ground.

"The bases are loaded," Casey said. "Chikorita, it's time for us to score!"

But Chikorita didn't have a chance to attack again.

A strange mechanical contraption came rolling across the field on wheels. Two giant metal arms held a huge baseball bat. The arms swung the bat wildly.

"What's going on?" Ash asked Casey. "Did you set this up?"

"Don't play dumb," Casey shot back. "I'm sure you rigged it. You're the cheater, after all."

"What are you talking about?" Ash asked.

While Ash and Casey argued, the mechanical arms rolled toward Chikorita. The leaf Pokémon shook with fear. It couldn't move.

The mechanical arms got ready to swing the bat once more. . . .

"Pika!" Pikachu jumped in front of Chikorita, trying to protect it.

Ash turned at the sound of Pikachu's voice.

"No!" Ash shouted. He ran toward the machine.

He was too late.

The mechanical arms swung at Pikachu and Chikorita. The giant bat bounced into them. It sent them flying across the field like baseballs.

"Pikachu!" Ash cried.

It looked like the Pokémon were going to crash into the scoreboard.

Then, at the last second, a giant baseball mitt appeared from behind the board. Pikachu and Chikorita landed safely in the mitt.

Jessie, James, and Meowth appeared at the top of the scoreboard. James reached out and grabbed Pikachu and Chikorita.

Jessie grinned. "Score one for Team Rocket!" she said.

Team Ash vs. Team Rocket

"Why are those Electabuzz fans stealing our Pokémon?" asked Casey.

"They're not Electabuzz fans," Ash said. "They're Pokémon thieves."

Jessie and James whipped off their Electabuzz uniforms to reveal their white Team Rocket uniforms underneath.

"That's right," James said. "And if you had any taste, you'd be rooting for Team Rocket instead of a silly baseball team!"

"We'll never cheer for you," Ash said. "Give back Pikachu and Chikorita right now!"

Meowth held up a small remote control device. "Sorry, we can't do that," he said. "But we can give you phase two of our plan. You're guaranteed to have a ball!"

Meowth pressed a button on the remote. An automatic ball-throwing machine rolled out onto the field. Meowth pressed another button, and baseballs began to fly out of the machine.

"Hey!" Ash yelled. He dove and ducked, trying to escape the barrage of balls. From the corner of his eye, he saw Casey doing the same thing.

"We can beat these guys if we work together," Ash said.

Casey nodded. "I know all about teamwork. Let's do it!"

Casey ran to the dugout and picked up a baseball bat. She began to hit the baseballs right back at Team Rocket.

"These goody-goodies are beating us at our own game," complained Jessie as she dodged a baseball.

Meowth turned a dial on the remote control. "Don't worry. We're about to hit a home run!"

Baseballs flew out of the machine at a fast and furious rate. Casey couldn't bat them all.

Ash quickly threw two Poké Balls.

"Squirtle, Bulbasaur, I choose you!" Ash cried.

Light blazed, and two Pokémon appeared. Squirtle looked like a cute blue turtle. Bulbasaur was a blue-green Grass Pokémon with a plant bulb on its back.

Squirtle started grabbing baseballs and hurling them back at Team Rocket. Two green vines extended from Bulbasaur's plant bulb. Bulbasaur used the vines to grab and throw baseballs, too.

Casey followed Ash's lead. "Pidgey! Rattata! You're up!"

Pidgey and Rattata exploded out of their Poké Balls. Pidgey flew at Team Rocket, and Rattata raced across the field. Rattata jumped up onto the scoreboard. Together, Casey's two Pokémon slammed into Team Rocket.

"You're not playing fair!" James yelled as Pikachu and Chikorita fell from his grasp. "Somebody call an umpire!" The two Pokémon landed safely on the field.

Ash and Casey ran up to them.

"Why don't you two finish this game?" Ash suggested.

"That's right," Casey said. "Let's go for a double play!"

Pikachu and Chikorita looked at each other and smiled. Then they faced Team Rocket.

Jessie, James, and Meowth had fallen onto the baseball field. They were dazed and covered with dust.

Chikorita started with a Razor Leaf Attack. The leaf on top of its head began to twirl around. Sharp, green leaves flew out of the leaf and pummeled Team Rocket.

"*Pikachuuuuuuuuuu!*" Pikachu let loose with another sizzling electric blast.

"This game is called on account of *pain*," Meowth quipped.

But Ash and Casey weren't finished. "Double Tackle!" they called out together.

Pikachu and Chikorita sped toward the crumpled heap that was Team Rocket. The blow sent Jessie, James, and Meowth sailing across the sky.

"Looks like Team Rocket's blasting off again!" they shouted.

Ash and Casey gave each other a high five.

"We did it!" they said together.

Misty and Brock joined them on the field.

"You two make a good team," Misty said.

The smile left Casey's face. "It's my fault

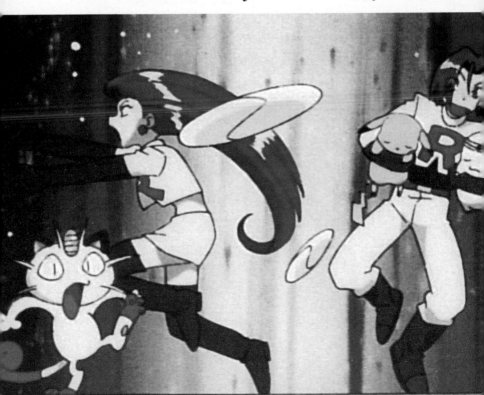

we had to fight those guys in the first place. I can't believe I let those crooks fool me. I need a lot more training."

"I need training just as much as you do," Ash said.

"You do?" Casey asked.

Ash smiled. "Sure. A good Pokémon trainer never stops learning."

Misty giggled. "Gosh, Ash. I thought you knew everything already."

Ash blushed. "Hey, I'm just being honest."

Ash turned back to Casey. "Anyway, I'm glad we battled again. It was cool seeing your Chikorita in action. I wish I had one."

"Chikorita are pretty common around here," Casey said. "Maybe you can catch one."

Ash eyed Casey's Chikorita. It really was a cool-looking Pokémon. And that Sweet Smell Attack was awesome.

"Who knows?" Ash said. "Maybe I will!"

5

The Wild Chikorita

"Now that your battle with Casey is over you can concentrate on the Johto League," Misty told Ash.

A few days had passed since they left Casey and her Chikorita. Ash, Misty, and Brock were headed down a new trail.

"I haven't stopped thinking about the Johto League," Ash said. "After all, that's the whole reason we're here."

In the Johto League, Ash could compete against other Pokémon trainers to get experience. First he'd have to challenge the lead-

ers of several Pokémon gyms. Then he could enter the Johto Tournament League. Only the best trainers won league matches. Ash hoped he would be one of them.

"I thought you were still thinking about that Chikorita," Misty teased. "You seemed really impressed by it."

"It had a lot of spirit," Ash said. "I wouldn't mind catching one."

Brock shivered. "I think the only thing we're going to catch around here is a cold," he said.

"It did get chilly all of a sudden," Ash agreed.

Misty pointed into the distance. "There's snow on those mountains. I bet there's some great snowboarding around here."

That sounded good to Ash. Snowboarding was a great way for Pokémon trainers to stay in shape.

Just then, Pikachu tugged on Ash's jeans. Ash looked down.

"Pika pi." Pikachu sniffed the air.

Ash sniffed, too. There was definitely a strange smell in the air. A sweet smell. There was something familiar about it . . .

"Chikorita!" Ash cried. He followed the smell off the trail.

There, behind a leafy bush, lay a wild Chikorita. The Pokémon was sprawled out in a patch of sunlight with its eyes closed.

"It looks like it's sunbathing," Misty remarked.

Ash took out Dexter. "Chikorita, the Leaf Pokémon, enjoys bathing in the sun's rays," confirmed the Pokédex.

Ash grabbed a Poké Ball from his belt. "This is great! I'm going to catch it."

Chikorita opened its eyes and hopped onto its feet. It glared at Ash.

"I think it heard you," Misty said.

The leaf on top of Chikorita's head started to spin around. The Grass Pokémon took a few bold steps toward Ash.

"This one's brave," Ash said. "No problem. Catching it will be a real challenge."

Ash threw the Poké Ball. "Bulbasaur, I choose you!" Ash cried.

Bulbasaur appeared in a flash of white light. Ash gave his first command.

"Bulbasaur, Vine Whip!"

The plant bulb on Bulbasaur's back opened, and two long, green vines shot out. Chikorita jumped up as soon as it saw the vines. But Bulbasaur was lightning-fast. It lashed at Chikorita with the vines.

Chikorita struck back quickly with a Razor Leaf Attack. A shower of sharp, green leaves assaulted Bulbasaur.

Bulbasaur responded with its own Razor Leaf Attack. It aimed its leaves at Chikorita's leaves, knocking them out of the way.

"Bulbasaur, Tackle!" Ash called out.

The Grass Pokémon charged after Chikorita. *Slam!* Bulbasaur made contact, and Chikorita toppled to the ground.

Ash made his move. He threw an empty Poké Ball at Chikorita.

"Go, Poké Ball!" yelled Ash.

But catching this Chikorita wasn't going to be easy. The Pokémon batted away the Poké Ball with the leaf on top of its head. Then it stared defiantly at Ash.

"I see. This Chikorita's stubborn," Ash said. "No problem. Bulbasaur, return!"

Bulbasaur disappeared inside its Poké Ball, and Ash threw out another one.

"Charizard, I choose you!"

The big Pokémon stomped its feet. Its flame burned brightly on the end of its tail.

Chikorita took one look at Charizard, lowered its head, and charged.

Charizard yawned and stuck out one huge foot. The move stopped Chikorita cold.

Then Charizard prepared for its attack. Its wings flapped furiously, and smoke came out of its nostrils.

But Chikorita moved fast. It attacked Charizard with Vine Whip. Chikorita's vines wrapped around Charizard's leg. Caught off guard, the lizard Pokémon fell to the ground with a thud.

"It caught you by surprise, Charizard!" Ash said.

Charizard hated to lose. It flew up into the air with Chikorita still attached to it. Charizard flew higher and higher, faster and faster. Chikorita swung dizzily on the vine.

Finally, Charizard landed. The vine came loose, and Chikorita collapsed in a heap.

"Oh, no!" Ash cried. "Are you okay?"

Chikorita stood up. It looked like it wanted to keep fighting.

Then it collapsed once more.

"I think we'd better take Chikorita to the Pokémon Center right away," Brock said.

Ash nodded. He knew Charizard didn't mean to give it such a hard time. He'd do anything to help Chikorita now.

"Let's go!" Ash said.

Nearby, Jessie, James, and Meowth watched the scene through binoculars.

"That Chikorita is something else," Jessie said. "It takes spunk to face Charizard head-on in battle. I'm impressed!"

"None of our Pokémon have any spunk," James said sadly.

Meowth frowned. "What about me?"

"That Chikorita's got more spunk in its big toe than you have in your whole body," Jessie sneered.

"Hey!" Meowth said. "That's not fair. But I have to admit I liked that Chikorita, too. Did you see how it stood up to that twerp? It's Team Rocket material."

"Then what are we waiting for?" James asked. "It's time to put Operation Chikorita into action!"

6

Kidnapped

The Pokémon Center was a log cabin nestled in the foot of the snowy mountains. Ash and the others rushed Chikorita up to the main desk.

A young woman in a nurse's uniform stood behind the desk. Every Pokémon Center had a nurse just like her. They were all named Joy, and all had red hair.

"It looks like your Chikorita needs some help," Nurse Joy said, smiling. "Don't worry. The Chikorita around here are very strong. It'll be fine in no time."

Ash relaxed. "That's great. You know, all my Pokémon could use a checkup. Can you take a look at them, too?"

"Sure," said Nurse Joy.

Ash handed her his Poké Balls. Brock and Misty decided to have their Pokémon checked, too.

Nurse Joy was about to carry away Chikorita when two doctors rushed into the Pokémon Center, pushing a stretcher. Each wore a long, white coat and a surgical mask.

"Step aside, step aside," said one of the doctors briskly. "I understand there's a Chikorita here that needs help."

"Uh, yes," said Nurse Joy. She seemed confused.

The other doctor scooped up Chikorita and plopped it onto the stretcher.

"Our emergency treatment center will handle this," said the doctor. Then both doctors quickly rushed out the door.

It happened so fast that Ash and the others barely had time to react. Ash rushed out after them. They were pushing the stretcher into the back of an ambulance.

"What are you doing with Chikorita?" Ash asked.

The doctors jumped inside the ambulance. Then they took off their surgical masks.

"Team Rocket!" Ash yelled.

Jessie and James grinned.

"This was easier than taking candy from a Togepi," Jessie said.

James tossed up a Poké Ball. "Weezing, Smog Attack!"

A foul-smelling Pokémon burst from the ball. Weezing looked like a purple cloud of

pollution with two heads. It immediately started spewing thick smog into the air.

The smog hit Ash right in the face. He coughed and choked, blinded by the stinky smoke.

As the smoke cleared, Ash heard the footsteps of the others behind him.

"Team Rocket has Chikorita," Ash said. "I'm going after them!"

"Pika!" Pikachu led the way, running down the road after the ambulance.

Ash could see the path the ambulance was taking up the mountain. He quickly ran off the trail, taking a shortcut to a rocky ledge. Pikachu followed his lead.

Ash and Pikachu reached the ledge just as Team Rocket drove underneath it.

"Jump!" Ash cried.

Ash and Pikachu leaped onto the roof of the ambulance.

"They don't know we're here," Ash whispered to Pikachu. "I'll just call on Charizard. We'll take care of this with one attack."

Ash reached for the Poké Balls on his belt.

And felt nothing.

"Oh, no," Ash wailed. "I left all my Poké Balls with Nurse Joy!"

Ash knew there was nothing he could do but wait — and plan.

The ambulance wound its way up the mountain. Finally, it reached a small cabin. Ash watched as Jessie, James, and Meowth walked inside. James carried Chikorita in his arms, and Chikorita didn't look too happy.

Ash shivered inside his vest. Snow covered the ground around them. The tree branches glistened with snow and icicles. He was in the middle of nowhere, without his Poké Balls. Nothing but snow.

Snow . . . Ash suddenly had an idea. He turned to Pikachu.

"We'll have to do our best with what we have," he told his Pokémon.

A few minutes later, Ash approached the cabin door. His pockets were stuffed with tightly packed snowballs.

Ash took a deep breath and kicked open the door.

"Prepare for trouble," Ash said, copying Team Rocket's motto. "No, make that double!"

Jessie and James sprang to their feet. They started to finish their motto.

"To protect the world from devastation. To unite all peoples within our nation," they chanted.

Ash interrupted them.

"To support the cause of truth and love.
To give the bad guys a great big shove.
A Pokémon Master is faster than light.
Surrender now, 'cause I know how to fight!"

"Pikachu!" added Pikachu.

"You stole our lines!" James whined.

"You're a thief," said Jessie. "That's what you are."

Ash whipped two snowballs out of his pockets. "You're the thieves! Take this!" Ash threw the snowballs at Team Rocket. He emptied his pockets, throwing snowballs as fast as he could.

"Hey, cut that out!" Jessie complained.

While Ash distracted Team Rocket, Pikachu rushed in and grabbed Chikorita. Pikachu and Chikorita escaped outside. When Ash saw that they were safe, he followed them.

"We did it!" Ash yelled.

The next thing he knew, he felt his feet slipping away beneath him.

Team Rocket had protected the camp by stringing a rope just above the ground. Ash, Pikachu, and Chikorita all tripped over the rope. They fell into a heap together. The force of the fall sent them rolling back down the mountain.

"Help!" Ash cried. Ash and the Pokémon rolled faster and faster. With each roll they picked up more snow until they became one big snowball.

Finally the snowball crashed into a tree. Ash opened his eyes, dazed.

He slowly sat up. Pikachu was right next to him. So was Chikorita. They both seemed as dazed as he was. He sighed, thankful they were all okay.

But it was getting dark. And a light snow was falling. They'd have to get somewhere safe. Soon.

"Come on guys," Ash said, standing up. "Let's get out of here."

Ash, Pikachu, and Chikorita walked through the trees. In the distance, Ash could see a small cave in the side of the mountain.

"Let's head over there," Ash said.

Pikachu followed Ash. But Chikorita stopped in its tracks.

Ash could tell Chikorita still didn't trust him.

"It's okay," Ash told it. "I'm not going to try to capture you. We need to get to that cave so we'll be safe."

But Chikorita didn't believe him.

"Chika!" The leaf Pokémon turned around and ran off into the woods.

"Pikachu?" Pikachu wondered what they should do.

49

"Let's go to the cave," Ash said, as snow piled on his shoulders. "Maybe Chikorita will change its mind."

Ash and Pikachu hurried to the cave. Ash found enough twigs and debris to make a small fire. The flame warmed his cold fingers and toes. But he didn't feel much better.

Ash looked out of the cave, and saw nothing but black sky and falling snow. There was no sign of Chikorita anywhere. Ash knew the Pokémon would freeze to death on its own.

He turned to Pikachu. "I've got to go after Chikorita," Ash said. "Stay here and keep warm. I'll be back as soon as I can."

And Ash ran out into the dark, snowy night.

7

Team Rocket Snowdown!

"Chikorita!" Ash called. "Chikorita!" The snow was falling hard and fast now. He tried not to think about how cold he was.

"Chikorita!" Ash didn't want to give up. He couldn't bear to think about the little Leaf Pokémon lost in the cold.

Suddenly, Ash felt his feet slip out from under him. He slid down a slippery snow-bank.

Ash landed facefirst in the snow. He struggled to his feet, brushing the snow from his eyes.

There, in front of him, was Chikorita.

The little Pokémon shivered in the cold. Tears streamed down its face.

"Chikorita, I'm so glad I found you!" Ash said. He held open his arms, and Chikorita jumped right in.

Ash hurried back to the cave. Pikachu cheered when it saw them. Ash quickly warmed Chikorita by the small fire. Then he bundled up Pikachu and Chikorita inside his vest.

"We'll get out of here in the morning," Ash

promised them. Pikachu and Chikorita nodded gratefully, and then closed their eyes.

Ash dozed off and on all night. He tried to keep the fire going as long as he could. When the first rays of sun shone into the cave, he smiled with relief.

"Wake up, guys," Ash said gently. "Let's find our way back to the Pokémon Center."

Pikachu and Chikorita squirmed out of Ash's vest and stretched. They walked to the cave entrance.

"Rise and shine, twerp!"

It was Jessie from Team Rocket! She, James, and Meowth were standing alongside some kind of strange contraption. It looked like a large box with a mechanical arm on each side.

Ash groaned. "What are you up to now?"

Meowth patted the contraption. "My newest invention will take care of you. My Snowball Buster will turn you all into snow cones!"

Ash tried to think of a plan. The mountain was behind them. Meowth's machine was in front of them. There was nowhere to run.

Meowth pressed a button on the machine.

"It's time for you to chill out, twerp!" said Jessie.

Jessie and James started shoveling snow into the box. Snowballs popped out of the top and landed in the mechanical hands. The machine's arms started lurching the snowballs at Ash, Pikachu, and Chikorita.

"Chikorita," Ash said, "are you up for a Razor Leaf Attack?"

Chikorita nodded. It looked angry. It stepped in front of Pikachu and Ash.

"Chika!" A barrage of leaves swirled from Chikorita's head. The leaves smacked into the attacking snowballs, deflecting them.

"Hey, that's *snow* fair!" complained Meowth.

"Now, Chikorita," Ash said, "bust that Snowball Buster!"

Chikorita aimed another attack of sharp leaves at the metal machine. The leaves sliced into the machine's gears. The Snowball Buster creaked and groaned.

The metal arms started throwing snowballs in the opposite direction. The snowballs bombarded Jessie, James, and Meowth.

"Meowth, you flake!" Jessie cried. "Your Snowball Buster is a bust!"

Ash turned to Pikachu. "Why don't you finish them off?"

"Pika!" Pikachu smiled happily. It faced Team Rocket. Sparks danced on its red cheeks.

"Pikachuuuuuuu!" Pikachu hurled a

Thunderbolt at Jessie, James, and Meowth. The attack sent them flying over the mountain.

"Looks like Team Rocket's blasting off again!" they cried.

Then another voice reached Ash's ears.

"Ash! You're alive!"

It was Misty. She, Brock, and Nurse Joy walked into view. They carried thick blankets and warm coats.

Misty threw a blanket over Ash. Brock scooped up Pikachu and Chikorita.

Ash told them all about their adventures as Nurse Joy led them back to the Pokémon Center. When they got there, Ash warmed up and ate a hot meal. Pikachu and Chikorita sat side by side, eating Pokémon food.

Ash sighed and turned to his friends. "We should get going. I want to cover some distance before night falls," he said.

Misty and Brock agreed. They collected their Poké Balls from Nurse Joy and got ready to hit the road once again.

Ash knelt down and spoke to Chikorita. "From now on, don't be too stubborn, okay?" Ash said. "Let people help you once in a while."

Chikorita nodded. It looked a little sad to see Ash go.

Ash and the others walked out of the Pokémon Center. They didn't get too far.

Chikorita ran out and sat down in front of Ash.

"Chika, chika," Chikorita rubbed against Ash's leg.

Misty smiled. "I think it likes you, Ash."

"Chikorita could use a trainer like you," Brock said. "It's got a lot of potential."

Ash looked at Chikorita. "What do you say, Chikorita? Would you like me to be your trainer?"

"Chika! Chika!" Chikorita said happily. It jumped up into Ash's arms.

"All right!" Ash cheered. "I caught a Chikorita."

Misty laughed. "Whatever you say, Ash."

Ash didn't care how he got Chikorita. He was happy Chikorita had chosen him.

Now his team of Pokémon was stronger than ever!

8

What's Wrong with Chikorita?

Ash couldn't wait to test Chikorita in a battle against another Pokémon trainer.

He soon had his chance.

On route to the next town, a young Pokémon trainer approached Ash, Misty, and Brock on the street. The boy eyed the Poké Balls hanging from Ash's belt.

"You're from out of town, huh?" asked the boy.

Ash nodded. "We came all the way from Pallet Town."

"My name's Nickey," the boy said. "I'm a Pokémon trainer, too. Want to battle?"

"Why not?" said Ash. Usually he looked for bigger challenges. But this was the perfect chance to try out his new Pokémon.

"Chikorita, I choose you!" Ash yelled. He threw a Poké Ball, and Chikorita landed gracefully on the grass.

"Come on out, Raticate!" Nickey cried. Raticate, the evolved form of Rattata, appeared in a flash of light. Raticate was larger

and fiercer than Rattata. It gave a little growl, revealing long, sharp teeth.

Ash and Nickey gave their first commands.

"Chikorita, Tackle!"

"Raticate, Hyper Fang!"

Chikorita lowered its head and raced toward Raticate. The Rat Pokémon ran at Chikorita, baring its two front fangs.

Raticate's fangs knocked into Chikorita. The leaf Pokémon toppled over.

"Raticate, Quick Attack!" yelled Nickey.

"Chikorita, Razor Leaf!" Ash shouted.

Chikorita jumped to its feet, but Raticate moved with lightning speed. It slammed into Chikorita again.

Ash knew Chikorita had been taken by surprise. This time, Chikorita struggled to get to its feet. It sent some razor-sharp leaves flying toward Raticate. But it was winded and weak. Ash had to get it out of there before Raticate could do any more damage.

Ash held out Chikorita's Poké Ball. "Good job, Chikorita. Return!"

Chikorita stood up, unsteady on its feet. It turned around and glared at Ash.

Then it charged at Raticate as fast it could. But Ash could see it was in no shape to fight. Raticate's next blow could be serious.

"Chikorita, return!" A red beam of light shot out of the Poké Ball.

Chikorita dodged the light.

"Chikorita, you can come back," Ash said. "I'm subbing in Pikachu."

Chikorita ignored Ash. It moved every time the light of the Poké Ball came near it.

"Hold still, Chikorita!"

But Chikorita wouldn't get back inside the ball. Ash didn't know what to do.

Then a woman's voice called out from a nearby house, "Nickey, time for dinner!"

Nickey held out a Poké Ball and recalled Raticate.

"Hey! We're not done with this battle," Ash said.

Nickey shrugged. "I've gotta get home. This battle wasn't going anywhere, anyway."

Nickey's words stung. Ash was a more experienced trainer; he should have been able to control Chikorita better than that.

"This is all your fault, Chikorita," Ash said under his breath.

Chikorita frowned and hung its head.

"This was only your first time using Chikorita in battle," Brock reminded Ash. "It's going to take a while before you get used to each other."

"Remember, it took you and Pikachu a while to learn to work together," Misty said.

Pikachu nodded. *"Pika, pika."*

Ash felt a little better. "You're right. You know, there's supposed to be a Pokémon Center a few blocks away. Let's go get something to eat."

"Sounds good to me," Misty said.

At the Pokémon Center, Ash, Misty, and Brock got some hot soup and sandwiches from the cafeteria. Brock took out some of his special Pokémon food. Ash released Squirtle, Bulbasaur, and Charizard from their Poké Balls. They greeted Pikachu, To-

gepi, and Chikorita while Brock fixed plates for all the Pokémon.

The Pokémon happily slurped up their food. All but Chikorita. The yellow Pokémon stared out a window, looking forlornly at the dark sky.

"Why don't you go eat with everyone else, Chikorita?" Ash said.

But Chikorita wouldn't even look at Ash.

Pikachu tried, too. It hopped up to Chikorita.

"Pika pika pi?" asked Pikachu. Ash knew it was asking Chikorita to join them.

Chikorita still didn't answer.

"That's odd," Brock remarked. "Chikorita's acting strangely."

"I think it's in a bad mood," said Misty.

Ash sighed. "Chikorita, you've got to tell me what's wrong!"

9

RunaWay Chikorita

"I think I can help you."

Ash turned. The voice belonged to Nurse Joy. Even though this Nurse Joy had red hair, she looked different from her counterparts in the other Pokémon Centers. She wore glasses and a blue lab coat instead of a nurse's uniform.

"I'm a Pokémon psychologist," Nurse Joy explained. "I specialize in Pokémon therapy."

"Ther-a-pee?" Ash asked. "Is that some kind of new Pokémon?"

Misty nudged Ash. "Therapy means medical care. She helps Pokémon with their problems, like if they're sad or depressed."

"Exactly," Nurse Joy said. "Your Chikorita is unhappy about something. I'll bet we can find out what it is. Why don't you and Chikorita join me for a session?"

Ash shrugged. "Sure." As a Pokémon trainer, he had to learn everything he could about Pokémon — even if it did seem strange.

Nurse Joy led them all into a small office. Chikorita still would not look at Ash. At

Nurse Joy's prodding, Ash told her all about how he had found Chikorita. He told her about the battle earlier, when he had tried to replace Chikorita with Pikachu.

Nurse Joy brightened. "That's it!" she cried. "Chikorita are very sensitive Pokémon. You hurt its feelings when you tried to replace it with Pikachu. Chikorita thinks you care more about Pikachu than you do for it."

"That's not true!" Ash said. He turned to Chikorita. "I just didn't want you to get hurt."

But Chikorita still sulked.

"What are we going to do?" Ash asked Nurse Joy.

Nurse Joy scribbled something on a notepad. "Chikorita needs to relax. There is a greenhouse next to the Pokémon Center that is the perfect environment for a Grass Pokémon. Let me keep it there overnight. I'm sure it will feel better by morning."

Ash looked at Misty and Brock.

"What do you think?" he asked.

Brock couldn't take his eyes off of Nurse Joy. He had a crush on every Nurse Joy he met. "It's a brilliant idea," Brock said. "Trust Nurse Joy."

"It couldn't hurt," Misty added.

Ash patted Chikorita's head. "I'll see you in the morning, Chikorita. I hope you feel better."

After Nurse Joy led Chikorita away, Ash, Misty and Brock returned to the lobby of the center. Ash called back his Pokémon, and climbed into his sleeping bag with Pikachu.

I hope Chikorita will be all right, Ash thought as he drifted off to sleep.

But Pikachu couldn't sleep. The Electric Pokémon slipped away from Ash. It crept outside of the Pokémon Center and walked over to the greenhouse.

Soft yellow light lit up the glass-walled greenhouse. Lush green plants seemed to cover every inch of space.

In the center, Pikachu spotted Chikorita

curled up on a green leaf. The Pokémon was sleeping fitfully.

Pikachu knew it could make Chikorita feel better. It opened the glass door.

Chikorita opened its eyes. It looked at Pikachu. Then it looked at the door.

"*Chika,*" Chikorita said sadly. Then it ran outside the open door.

Chikorita ran as fast as it could. It could hear Pikachu trying to catch up with it.

Chikorita veered off the dirt road and into a grassy field. It felt comfortable there, and it knew it could lose Pikachu.

Chikorita ran and ran. The sound of Pikachu's footsteps died away. Chikorita stopped, panting.

A bright moon shone on a worn-down warehouse that sat at the edge of the field. It looked like a good hiding place. Chikorita walked through the open doors.

A beam of moonlight poured through a hole in the ceiling. Chikorita could see dusty wooden crates stacked on top of one another. Chikorita hopped on a crate and soaked in a moonbeam. Normally, the leaf Pokémon loved sunlight best, but moonlight felt good, too.

Then something blocked out the light. Strange, dark shadows loomed on the floor.

Chikorita looked up. Four tough-looking Fighting Pokémon had stepped out on top of some crates. They stared at Chikorita, and they didn't look happy.

Chikorita sized up the Pokémon.

There was Hitmonlee. This Pokémon had

two large eyes, but no nose or mouth. Its strong legs delivered powerful kicks.

Next to Hitmonlee stood Hitmonchan. It had broad shoulders, and wore two red boxing gloves. A blow from this Pokémon's fists was not easy to recover from.

Beside Hitmonchan, Machoke flexed its strong arms. This gray Pokémon had bulging muscles all over its body. It wore a gold belt around its waist, like a weight lifter.

The leader of the group seemed to be a Primeape. This round-bodied Pokémon looked like a cross between a monkey and a pig. It walked on two legs, and wore brown boxing gloves. Its bad temper made Primeape a tough fighter.

Primeape made the first move. It jumped off the crate, and aimed right for Chikorita.

The leaf Pokémon moved fast. Two vines whipped out of its neck and expertly lassoed Primeape in midair. Chikorita tossed Primeape into a stack of wooden crates. The crates shattered around it, covering it in splintered wood.

Chikorita took a deep breath. It turned

back to the three remaining Pokémon. Which would make the next move?

Hitmonlee, Hitmonchan, and Machoke jumped down to the floor at the same time.

Chikorita braced itself. Could it take on all three at once?

"Hitmonlee."

"Hitmonchan."

"Machoke!"

The three Pokémon bowed down in front of Chikorita. The leaf Pokémon had beat their leader. They would show it the proper respect.

Chikorita smiled. Then it jumped down onto the floor and walked toward the Fighting Pokémon.

A tiny voice made Chikorita stop.

"Pika?"

Pikachu stood in the doorway of the warehouse. The Fighting Pokémon looked at Chikorita. Did Chikorita want them to fight the new Pokémon?

Chikorita looked at the Fighting Pokémon. It looked at Pikachu.

And it made its decision.

10

The Recycled Robot

Morning brought pandemonium to the Pokémon Center.

Ash couldn't believe that Pikachu and Chikorita were both missing. Ash, Brock, and Misty huddled behind Nurse Joy, who sat at a video monitor. She studied film from the security cameras, trying to find out what happened.

"Look here," she said.

Ash watched the video as Chikorita escaped from the greenhouse. Pikachu chased it, and then they both disappeared from view.

"We've got to find them," Ash said.

Nurse Joy nodded. "Be careful," she said. "There are some pretty tough Pokémon in this neighborhood."

Misty and Brock followed Ash out of the Pokémon Center. Ash felt panicked. He had to find Pikachu and Chikorita before something bad happened.

"Pikachu! Chikorita!" Ash yelled.

"They could be anywhere Ash," Misty said. "We need to think of a plan."

Brock looked thoughtful. "Bulbasaur is a Grass Pokémon like Chikorita. Maybe it can follow Chikorita's Sweet Scent."

"That's a great idea!" Ash said. He tossed Bulbasaur's Poké Ball.

The blue-green Pokémon appeared in front of Ash.

"Bulbasaur, follow Chikorita's scent," Ash said.

Bulbasaur sniffed at the grass. It turned around. Then it started to walk forward, sniffing all the way.

Ash and the others followed Bulbasaur

into a grassy field. Soon Ash saw a run-down warehouse up ahead.

Inside the warehouse, he spotted a light-green Pokémon.

"Chikorita!" Ash cried. He ran toward the warehouse. But where was Pikachu?

"Pika!" Pikachu stepped out of the warehouse. It smiled and waved to Ash.

"It looks like Chikorita and Pikachu are trying to become friends," Brock remarked.

Ash sighed with relief. Pikachu and Chikorita were all right. Even better, they seemed to be getting along.

He thought all his troubles were over.

"Prepare for trouble!" a voice cried.

Ash groaned. Those words could only mean one thing.

Jessie and James burst down from the ceiling of the warehouse. They landed right behind Pikachu and Chikorita.

"Hi, twerp," Jessie called out to Ash. "We hear you're having a sale on cute Pokémon today."

"That's right," James said. "They're a great price. Free!" He and Jessie reached down to grab Pikachu and Chikorita.

"No!" Ash cried. He charged toward the warehouse.

At the same time, four Fighting Pokémon jumped out and surrounded Jessie and James. Ash recognized Hitmonlee, Hitmon-chan, Machoke, and Primeape.

These must be the tough Pokémon Nurse Joy was talking about, Ash realized.

But Jessie and James didn't look afraid.

Next to the warehouse, a hot-air balloon descended from the sky and hung in midair. The balloon had a Meowth face on it, and Meowth piloted the balloon. Team Rocket's Pokemon whipped out a remote control device and pressed a button.

"Save your punches for this guy," Meowth told the Fighting Pokémon.

The ground shook. Ash looked up. A giant creature stomped toward the warehouse.

It looked like some kind of robot. Tires piled up together to make two huge legs, a thick body, and powerful arms. Metal hubcaps on its face looked like eyes. A small satellite·dish sat on top of its head.

"It's recycled," Meowth said proudly. "It saves us money, and it's good for the environment, too!"

Jessie grinned. "I never get *tired* of your ideas. But does it work?"

"Just watch," Meowth said. It lowered two ropes down from the balloon.

Jessie and James each grabbed onto a rope. At the same time, the Fighting Pokémon ran out of the warehouse and attacked the robot. One by one, they charged with all their might.

One by one, the robot smacked them away with its mighty fists.

Chikorita frowned, angry that its friends were hurt. It ran toward the robot. The giant creature tried to stomp on Chikorita, but it dodged every attempt.

Pikachu ran to help Chikorita.

"Pikachuuuuuu!" Pikachu let loose with a sizzling electric blast. The Thunderbolt ripped into the robot.

Nothing happened.

"That's another great thing about my masterpiece," Meowth said. "Rubber absorbs electricity. It's pika-proof!"

The robot reached down and grabbed

Pikachu in one hand. Chikorita tried to stop it by shooting sharp razor leaves. The robot didn't even feel the attack. It reached down and scooped up Chikorita in the other hand.

"It's been nice doing business with you," Jessie said. "We'll be going now. And we're taking Pikachu and Chikorita with us!"

11

Robot Rescue

"No!" Ash yelled. He had to do something. But all his Pokémon put together couldn't fight that robot.

Brock tapped him on the shoulder. He pointed to the top of the robot's head.

"That satellite dish is a radio receiver. That's how they're controlling it," Brock said. "If you could break that . . ."

Ash nodded. "I'll do it. And I know just how to get up there, too. Heracross, I choose you!"

Ash threw a Poké Ball, and a large Bug

Pokémon popped out. Heracross was about as tall as Ash. It had the shiny brown armor of a beetle, and a curved horn on top of its head shaped like a half-moon.

"Heracross, I need you to use your horn throw for me," Ash said.

Misty stepped in front of him. "Hold on, Ash. That's too dangerous."

"I know," Ash said. "But I have no choice. Pikachu and Chikorita are my friends."

"*Heracross!*" Heracross wanted to help, too. It lowered its head, and Ash climbed into the curved horn.

Heracross threw back its head and sent Ash flying up toward the robot. Ash took off as if he were propelled by a slingshot. He flew up, up toward the satellite dish . . .

. . . and missed. He landed back on the ground on top of a soft pile of rubber tires.

Brock and Misty ran up to him. "Are you okay?" Misty asked.

Ash felt sore, but that was about it. "I can't believe I missed. I've got to get up there somehow."

Ash anxiously followed the robot. It stomped across the field, still holding Pikachu and Chikorita. Team Rocket's balloon flew by it. Ash saw that the robot was about to pass a tall water tower.

"That's it!" Ash cried. He ran to the water tower and climbed up the ladder as fast as he could.

The robot stomped by. Ash leaned over. The satellite dish was in his reach . . .

"Not so fast!" Meowth said from above. It

pressed a button, and the robot took a sharp turn.

"Whoa!" Ash lost his balance and toppled over the side of the tower. His stomach sank as he plummeted to the ground below. He closed his eyes, waiting for the impact.

It never came. Ash felt two strong vines wrap around his waist. He opened his eyes. Chikorita had saved him. The Pokémon pulled Ash up to the robot's hand.

"Thanks, Chikorita," Ash said. "Now lift me up to that satellite dish."

The vines carried Ash to the top of the robot's head. Ash trembled as the robot stomped across the field. Ash tried not to look down. He only needed a few seconds.

Ash grabbed the metal dish and twisted with all his might.

"Time to put on the brakes," Ash said, as he pulled the satellite dish apart.

The robot began to twitch and shake uncontrollably. Ash tumbled off of the robot's head. Luckily, Chikorita's vines still held him tight.

Ash managed to land on his feet in the

grass. He looked up. The robot was doing some kind of crazy dance.

"Do something, Meowth!" Jessie snapped. She and James still clung to ropes hanging from the balloon.

Meowth pressed every button on the remote. "I can't control it!"

The robot unclenched its hands, and Pikachu and Chikorita tumbled to the ground below. Ash scooped them up and ran back to Brock and Misty.

From a safe distance, Ash watched as the robot waved its arms wildly. It looked like it was going to tear up the balloon.

Meowth bared its sharp claws. "Sorry guys," it told Jessie and James. "You're weighing me down. It's time for this cat to fly!"

Meowth reached down and sliced through the ropes holding Jessie and James. The two villains fell to the ground — and landed on the robot's head, right on top of the satellite dish.

Sparks flew from the mangled metal. Ash saw what looked like a flash of flame, and then there was an explosion.

The robot lifted off the ground like a rocket. It crashed into the balloon. Jessie, James, and Meowth went careening across the sky.

"Looks like we're blasting off again!" Meowth cried.

Ash hugged Pikachu and Chikorita.

"I'm so glad you're both okay," Ash said. "I don't know what I would have done without you."

Both Pokémon smiled.

Ash looked at Chikorita. "I'm sorry you ran away, Chikorita," he said. "You're an important part of my team. Pikachu and I need you. Right, Pikachu?"

"Pika!" Pikachu nodded.

Chikorita looked happy. *"Chikorita!"* said the Pokémon.

Ash grinned. He looked at his friends.

"Our team can't be beat," Ash said. "Let's get moving to the next town. I've got to compete in the Johto League!"